Paddington
Goes for
Gold

First published in hardback in Great Britain by HarperCollins Children's Books in 2012

1 3 5 7 9 10 8 6 4 2

ISBN: 978-0-00-742772-7

HarperCollins Children's Books is a division of HarperCollins Publishers Ltd.

Text copyright © Michael Bond 2012
Illustrations copyright © R. W. Alley 2012

Visit our website at: www.harpercollins.co.uk

Printed and bound in China

MICHAEL BOND

Paddington
Goes for
Gold

illustrated by R.W. ALLEY

HarperCollins *Children's Books*

One morning Paddington was lingering by the Browns' front door at number thirty-two Windsor Gardens in case a postcard arrived from his Aunt Lucy in Peru, when to his surprise a leaflet came through the letter box and landed on his nose.

Paddington didn't normally take much notice of leaflets, and he was about to throw it in the nearest waste bin when the words FREE ENTRY and PRIZES caught his eye. It sounded much more interesting than usual, so he decided to show the leaflet to Mr Brown when he came home from work that evening.

"It's from the local sports club," explained Mr Brown over dinner that evening. "They're holding a fund-raising event tomorrow. There's something for everyone, and prizes galore."

"There's even a knitting competition," announced Paddington, for Mrs Bird's benefit.

The Browns' housekeeper gave a non-committal grunt.

"Let's go, Dad," chorused Jonathan and Judy. "It sounds fun."

"Well…" began Mr Brown. "I was picturing a round of golf."

"I'll iron your shorts, Henry," said Mrs Brown. "They could do with an airing."

"If they still fit me," said Mr Brown gloomily.

The Browns set off in high spirits early the next day, but it was short-lived, for as they entered the sports ground the first person they bumped into was Mr Curry. Their next-door neighbour could put a damper on anything.

Worse still, he was making a beeline for Paddington.

"I suppose it had to happen," murmured Mr Brown. "That leaflet must have gone to all the houses in the area."

"Hold this ball for a moment, bear," boomed Mr Curry, thrusting a round object into Paddington's paws.

Mr Curry roared with laughter as Paddington staggered backwards.

"Caught you out for once, bear," he chuckled. "It's made of lead and it's used for what's called Putting the Shot. You're supposed to throw it as hard as you can."

Mrs Bird took a firm grip of her handbag, but she had no need of it, for Mr Curry suddenly gave a roar of pain.

"Bear!" he bellowed, hopping on one leg. "What do you think you're doing?"

"You said I was supposed to throw it," exclaimed Paddington. "I'm afraid it didn't go very far."

"Far enough to land on my foot. I don't forget things in a hurry!" cried Mr Curry.

"No prizes there, I'm afraid," called a steward, joining the group. "Anyone for the three-legged race? You'd better hurry. It's about to start."

Jonathan and Judy made a dash for it, closely followed by Paddington, only too anxious to escape Mr Curry's wrath.

"But you've got four legs between you," Paddington hissed. "Two and two makes four."

"Don't worry," Judy removed her ribbon. "If we tie two of them together that makes three."

"Leave it to me," said Paddington. "Bears are good at knots."

"Ready…" called the starter. "Steady… Go!"

Jonathan tore off straight away, but Judy was unable to move.

"Oh dear," said Paddington. "I think I must have tied the wrong two legs together by mistake."

"No prizes there either I'm afraid," said the steward. He turned to Mr Brown. "Shall I put you down for the hundred metre hurdles?"

"Actually," said Mr Brown, "I rather fancy the slow bicycle race. I used to be a dab hand at it when I was a boy."

"I'm for the knitting competition," said Mrs Bird. "I've brought my own needles."

"Good, good," said the steward. He turned to Mrs Brown. "And you, dear lady?"

"I want to keep an eye on my husband," said Mrs Brown firmly.

Paddington found it hard to see what was going on when he
joined the crowd at the start of the race, but he pricked up
his ears when he heard Mrs Brown say she was worried Mr
Brown might fall off his bicycle.

"He's going ever so slowly," agreed Judy.

"Leave it to me, everybody!" called Paddington. And he
ran on to the track as fast as he could.

"Don't worry, Mr Brown," he called. "I'm here!"

Grasping the bicycle saddle with both paws he pushed with all his might and Mr Brown sailed past all the other contestants in a flash.

"Why ever did you do that?" cried Mr Brown. "The last one past the tape is first in a slow bicycle race. I could have been a contender."

"I'm sorry, Mr Brown," gasped Paddington. "I thought it was a funny name for a race, but we didn't have them in Darkest Peru."

"Don't worry, Dad," called Jonathan from a nearby tent. "Wait until you see Mrs Bird's knitting. She's on a winning streak."

"Look at her needles," agreed Judy. "They're going like windmills. I hope she doesn't do herself a mischief."

"I expect she could do with a marmalade sandwich," said Paddington. "I brought some specially."

"Don't stop, Mrs Bird," he called. "I'm coming!"

The Browns' housekeeper had her hands full, so he popped a sandwich into her open mouth.

Mrs Bird gave a gurgle, but she didn't slow down.

"That's torn it," said Judy. "If Mrs Bird gets marmalade over her needles she won't be pleased."

"It's probably against the rules to feed competitors," said Mr Brown.

Jonathan gave a groan. "What's Paddington up to now?" he said.

"I've found some more wool if you run out, Mrs Bird," called Paddington.

"Grrr! Grrr!" spluttered Mrs Bird, shaking her head violently. "Grrr! Grrr!"

Paddington set to work. He had his back to Mrs Bird, so he didn't notice that as he wound the wool into a ball her piece of knitting grew smaller and smaller.

"Grrrrr!" said Mrs Bird. "Grrrrrrr! Grrrrrrrrrrr!"

"How on earth did he manage to do that?" asked Mr Brown.

"Don't even ask, Henry," replied Mrs Brown.

"Bang goes our last chance of a prize!" groaned Judy.

"We can't give up now," said Jonathan. "They're getting ready for the relay race. Who's for making up a foursome?"

Paddington's paw shot up. Judy raised her hand, and after a moment Mr Brown joined them.

"In for a penny, in for a pound," he said.

Judy made the first circuit of the track…

before passing the baton to Jonathan…

who in turn passed it to Paddington…
"Whatever you do," he gasped, "don't drop it."

Mr Brown was ready and waiting as a familiar figure rounded the bend.

"Where is it?" he cried, as Paddington drew alongside him. "The baton… where is it?"

"I don't know, Mr Brown," gasped Paddington. "I had it when I left."

"You had it when you left?" repeated Mr Brown. "What do you mean… you had it when you left?"

Paddington did his best to think of another way of saying it. "Jonathan told me not to drop it…" he said. "So I put it somewhere for safe keeping."

"I don't believe it," groaned Mr Brown.

As the race came to an end everybody cheered and began
waving their hats in the air, so Paddington joined in.

"There it is!" cried Mrs Brown, pointing at Paddington's head.
"It was under his hat all the time."

"I remember now," said Paddington.

"Don't be cross, Henry," said Mrs Brown. "It isn't as though
he dropped it."

"Cross?" repeated Mr Brown. "Have you seen it? I'm thankful
he *didn't* give it to me. It's covered
in marmalade. Ugh! I think
it's time we went home."

As the Browns were leaving, a man on the gate handed Paddington an envelope. "It's a small 'thank you'," he said. "You are our very first bear contestant and you seem to have brought us luck. Visitors have been flooding in."

The envelope contained a medal made of gold foil, and it had a ribbon attached so that Paddington could hang it round his neck. There was some writing across the front, but he was too excited to read it.

"I think," he announced, "I shall show it to Mr Curry. "It might make his leg better."

"Mr Curry doesn't deserve it…" began Mrs Bird.

But Paddington was already on his way, and by the time they caught up with him all they heard was a cry of "Bear!", followed by a loud bang.

"Whatever happened?" asked Judy, as Paddington reappeared.

"Well," said Paddington, "when I showed Mr Curry my medal he started hopping about on one leg, but it was the wrong one, and when I mentioned it he slammed the door in my face."

"It's a pity you didn't mention the words on the front of the medal," said Mr Brown. "*Winning isn't everything. Taking part and doing your best is what matters most.*"

"I would rather someone else did that," said Paddington politely. I don't think Mr Curry likes my mentions."

"After you, Henry," said Mrs Brown amid laughter all round.